Thomas Jones

The Experience of Thomas H. Jones

A Slave For Forty-Three Years

Thomas Jones

The Experience of Thomas H. Jones
A Slave For Forty-Three Years

ISBN/EAN: 9783744733052

Printed in Europe, USA, Canada, Australia, Japan

Cover: Foto ©Raphael Reischuk / pixelio.de

More available books at **www.hansebooks.com**

TAYLOR-ADAMS BOSTON.

THE EXPERIENCE

OF

TH**** S H. JONES,

WHO WAS

SLAVE

F**** TY-THREE Y****

***

EN BY A FR*

TO HIM BY BRO***

BOSTON:
PRINTED BY BAZIN & CHANDLER, 37 CORNHILL.
1862.

A suffering brother would affectionately present this simple story of deep personal wrongs to the earnest friends of the Slave. He asks you to buy and read it, for, in so doing, you will help one who needs your sympathy and aid, and you will receive, in the perusal of this simple narrative, a more fervent conviction of the necessity and blessedness of toiling for the desolate members of the one great brotherhood who now suffer and die, ignorant and despairing, in the vast prison land of the South. "Whatsoever ye would that men should do to you, do ye even so to them."

THOMAS H. JONES.

TO THE FRIENDS OF SUFFERING HUMANITY.

The undersigned take pleasure in certifying, that they have formed an acquaintance with Brother **Thomas Jones**, since his escape from Slavery : having seen and perused his letters, and his certificates of Church relations, and made all suitable inquiries, most cordially recommend him to the confidence and aid of all who have a heart to sympathize with a down trodden and outraged portion of the great brotherhood. We would also say, that we have heard brother Jones lecture before our respective churches, and we only speak the unanimous sentiments of our people, when we say, that his narrative is one of thrilling interest, calculated to secure the attention of any audience, and to benefit the sympathizing hearts of all who will make themselves acquainted with the present condition and past experience of this true-hearted brother.

· E. A. STOCKMAN,
Pastor of the Wesleyan Church, Boston.

DANIEL FOSTER,
Pastor of the Free Evangelical Church,
North Danvers, Mass.

To whom it may concern :—This may certify, that the bearer, Thomas Jones, has lectured to my people, with good success, giving a satisfaction uncommon to one deprived, as he has been, of moral or mental cultivation.

I can cheerfully recommend him to all such as may be inclined to give him a hearing or assistance in any way, in confidence, feeling that he is an honest and upright man.

A. B. FLANDERS,
Pastor of W. M. Church, Exeter, N H.

Nov. 25, 1849.

TESTIMONIALS.

BOSTON, MARCH 29, 1851.

In consequence of the passage of the Fugitive Slave Law, at the last session of Congress, a general flight from the country of all fugitive slaves in the Northern States has become necessary as a matter of personal safety. Among the number thus compelled to leave is the bearer of this, Thomas H. Jones, a Wesleyan preacher, and pastor of a colored church in the neighboring city of Salem, who carries with him a narrative of his life for sale. My personal acquaintance with him is limited ; but those among my friends who know him intimately speak of him as a most worthy man, and one peculiarly entitled to the sympathy and aid of those who love God and regard man. Though he is a man, "created a little lower than the angels"— exemplary in life — a servant and minister of Jesus Christ — in all the United States there is not a spot on which he can stand in safety from pursuing bloodhounds, and must flee to England to prevent being again reduced to the condition of a beast ! May the God of the oppressed raise him up many friends abroad !

WM. LLOYD GARRISON.

LYNN, JAN. 17, 1859.

I have been for several years well acquainted with the bearer of this note, Rev. Thomas H. Jones, and it is a pleasure to me to recommend him cordially to all who love God, humanity and freedom. He was forty-three years a slave, but by great courage, industry and perseverance, has fought his way to freedom of body and spirit, and has devoted himself with fidelity and success to the spiritual salvation of men. He has a family, part free and part yet in bonds, whose wants roll heavy responsibilities on him as a husband and father, and is therefore obliged to toil hard for daily bread. I bespeak for him the sympathy and benevolence of the public as an earnest, honest Christian man, worthy of all confidence that he may claim, and of all assistance that he may solicit.

FALES H. NEWHALL, Pastor of South St., M. E. Church.

WILMINGTON, APRIL 25, 1857.

I am personally acquainted with Rev. Thomas H. Jones, a fugitive from Slavery. During the past two years have heard him preach and lecture to large congregations with much acceptance.

Br. Jones is a warm-hearted Christian and a worthy Minister of Jesus Christ. It will do any people good to hear him tell the "Story of his wrongs,"

ORIGEN SMITH, Pastor of the Baptist Church in Dover, Vt.

GREENWICH, MARCH 9, 1857.

This may certify that Mr. Thos. Jones, a fugitive from Southern bondage, lectured to us last evening in a very acceptable manner, and enlisted the interest and sympathy of the people in no ordinary degree. He is a true man and a beloved brother and fellow laborer in the Lord. He leaves behind him in his departure a pleasant impression, both in the family and in public. He is hereby commended to the kind regards and friendly aid of all who love the Divine Redeemer, and have sympathy with the oppressed.

E. P. BLODGETT.

NARRATIVE OF A REFUGEE SLAVE.

I was born a slave. My recollections of early life are associated with poverty, suffering and shame. I was made to feel, in my boyhood's first experience, that I was inferior and degraded, and that I must pass through life in a dependent and suffering condition. The experience of forty-three years, which were passed by me in slavery, was one of dark fears and darker realities. John Hawes was my first master. He lived in Hanover County, N. C., between the Black and South Rivers, and was the owner of a large plantation, called Hawes' Plantation. He had over fifty slaves. I remained with my parents nine years. They were both slaves, owned by John Hawes. They had six children, Richard, Alexander, Charles, Sarah, myself, and John. I remember well that dear old cabin, with its clay floor and mud chimney, in which, for nine years, I enjoyed the presence and love of my wretched parents.

Father and mother tried to make it a happy place for their dear children. *They* worked late into the night many and many a time to get a little simple furniture for their home and the home of their children; and they spent many hours of willing toil to stop up the chinks between the logs of their poor hut, that they and their children might be protected from the storm and the cold. I can testify, from my own painful experience, to the deep and fond affection which the slave cherishes in his heart for its home and its dear ones. We have no other tie to link us to the human family, but our fervent love for those who are *with* us and of us in relations of sympathy and devotedness, in wrongs and wretchedness. My dear parents were conscious of the desperate and incurable woe of their position and destiny; and of the lot of inevitable suffering in store for their beloved children. They talked about our coming misery, and they lifted up their voices and wept aloud, as they spoke of our being torn from them and sold off to the dreaded slave-trader, perhaps never again to see them or hear from them a word of fond love. I have heard them speak of their willingness to bear their own sorrows without complaint, if only we, their dear children, could be safe from the wretchedness before us. And I remember, and *now* fully understand, as I did not *then*, the sad and tearful look they would fix upon us when we were gathered round them and running on with our foolish prattle. I am a father, and I have had the same feelings of unspeakable anguish, as I have looked upon my precious babes, and have thought of the ignorance, degradation and woe which they must endure as slaves. The great God, who knoweth all the secrets of the heart, and He only, knows the bitter sorrow I now feel when I think of my four dear children who are slaves, torn from me and consigned to hopeless servitude by the iron hand of ruthless wrong. I love those children with all a father's fondness. God gave them to me; but my brother took them from me, in utter scorn of a father's earnest pleadings; and I never shall look upon them again, till I meet them and my oppressors at the final gathering. Will not the Great Father and God make them and me reparation in the final award of mercy to the victim, and of Justice to the cruel desolator?

Mr. Hawes was a very severe and cruel master. He kept no overseer, but managed his own slaves, with the help of Enoch, his oldest son. Once a year he distributed clothing to his slaves. To the men he gave one pair of shoes, one blanket, one hat, and five yards of coarse, homespun cotton; to the women a corresponding outfit, and enough to make one frock for each of the children. The slaves were obliged to make up their own clothes, after the severe labor of the plantation had been performed. And other clothing, beyond this yearly supply, which they might need, the slaves were compelled to get by extra work, or do without.

The supply of food given out to the slaves, was one peck of corn a week, or some equivalent, and nothing besides. They must grind their own corn, after the work of the day was performed, at a mill which stood on the plantation. We had to eat our coarse bread without meat, or butter, or milk. Severe labor alone gave us an appetite for our scanty and unpalatable fare. Many of the slaves were so hungry after their excessive toil, that they were compelled to steal food in addition to this allowance.

During the planting and harvest season, we had to work early and late. The men and women were called at three o'clock in the morning, and were worked on the plantation till it was dark at night. After that they must prepare their food for supper and for the breakfast of the next day, and attend to other duties of their own dear homes. Parents would often have to work for their children at home, aftereach day's protracted toil, till the middle of the night, and then snatch a few hours' sleep, to get strength for the heavy burdens of the next day.

In the month of November, and through the winter season, the men and women worked in the fields, clearing up new land, chopping and burning bushes, burning tar kilns, and digging ditches. They worked together, poorly clad, and suffering from the bitter cold and wet of those winter months. Women, wives and mothers, daughters and sisters, on that plantation, were compelled to toil on cold, stormy days in the open field, while the piercing wind and driving storm benumbed their limbs, and almost froze the tears that came forth out of their cold and desolate hearts. Little boys, and girls, too, worked and cried, toting brush to the fires, husking the corn, watching the stock, and running on errands for master and mistress, and their three sons, Enoch, Edward and John, and constantly receiving from them scoldings and beatings as their reward.

Thus passed nine years of my life ; years of suffering, the shuddering memory of which is deeply fixed in my heart.   Oh, that these happy, merry boys and girls, whom I have seen in Massachusetts since my escape from slavery, whom I have so often met rejoicing in their mercies since I came here, only knew the deep wretchedness of the poor slave child !   For then, I am sure, their tender hearts would feel to love and pray for these unhappy ones, on whose early life hopeless sufferings bear down a crushing, killing burden !. These nine years of wretchedness passed, and a change came for me.   My master sold me to Mr. Jones, of Wilmington, N. C., distant forty-five miles from Hawes' plantation.   Mr. Jones sent his slave driver, a colored man named Abraham, to conduct me to my new home in Wilmington.   I was at home with my mother when he came.   He looked in at the door, and called to me,

" Tom, you must go with me."   His looks were ugly, and his voice was savage.   I was very much afraid, and began to cry, holding on to my mother's clothes, and begging her to protect me, and not let the man take me away.   Mother wept bitterly, and in the midst of her loud sobbings, cried out in broken words, " I can't save you, Tommy ; master has sold you, you must go."   She threw her arms around me, and while the hot tears fell on my face, she strained me to her heart.   There she held me, sobbing and mourning, till the brutal Abraham came in, snatched me away, hurried me out of the house where I was born, my only home, and tore me away from the dear mother who loved me as no other friend could do.   She followed him, imploring a moment's delay, and weeping aloud, to the road, where he turned around, and striking at her with his heavy cowhide, fiercely ordered her to stop bawling, and go back into the house.

Thus was I snatched from the presence of my loving parents, and from the true affection of the dear ones of home.   For thirteen weary years did my heart turn in its yearning for that precious home.   And then at the age of twenty-two, was I permitted to revisit my early home. I found it all desolate; the family all broken up; father was sold and gone; Richard, Alexander, Charles, Sarah and John, were sold and gone. Mother prematurely old, heart-broken, utterly desolate, weak and dying, alone remained. I saw her, and wept once more on her bosom. I went back to my chains with a deeper woe in my heart than I had ever felt before. There was but one thought of joy in my wretched consciousness, and that was, that my kind and precious mother would soon be at rest in the grave. And then, too, I remember, I mused with deep earnestness on death, as the only friend the poor slave had. And I wished that I too, might lie down by my mother's side, and die with her in her loving embrace.

I should have related, that one of the earliest scenes of painful memory associated with my opening years of suffering, is connected with a severe whipping which my master inflicted on my sister Sarah. He tied her up, having compelled her to strip herself entirely naked, in the smoke house, and gave her a terrible whipping—at least so it seemed to my young heart, as I heard her scream, and stood by my mother, who was wringing her hands in an agony of grief, at the cruelties which her tender child was enduring. I do not know what my sister had done for which she was then whipped : but I remember that her body was marked and scarred for weeks after that terrible scourging, and that our parents always after *seemed* to hold their breath when they spoke of it. Sarah was the last of the family who was sold ; and my poor mother never looked up after this final act of cruelty was accomplished. I think of my only sister now ; and often try to imagine *where* she is, and *how* she fares in this cruel land of slavery. And, oh, my God, how dark and wretched are these pictures! Can I think of that poor sister without a sorrow too great for utterance ? Ah me! how can the generous, loving brother or sister, blessed with freedom, forget the cruel sorrows and wrongs of the slave brother

1*

and sister ? How fellowship, even in the least act of comity, the atrocious slave-holder ? There may be some who do this from ignorance of such cruel wrongs. God grant this simple story may enlighten some who only need to *know* our deep necessities, to give us their willing sympathy and aid and love.

My journey to Wilmington with the heartless Abraham was a very sad one. We walked all the way. I was afraid of my savage companion ; and yet my heart felt so desolate, and my longings for sympathy so intense, that I was impelled to turn to my cruel guide for relief. He was striding along in stern gloom and silence too fast for my young feet to keep pace ; and I began to feel that I *must* stop and rest. It was bitter cold, too, and I was poorly clad to bear the keen air of a January day. My limbs were weary with travel, and stiff with cold. I could not go on at the rate I had done, and so I turned to my guide and begged him to take me into some hut and let me rest and get warm. He cursed me, and told me to keep silence and come along, or he would warm me with a cowhide. Oh, I thought how cruel and hopeless my lot! Would that I could fall down here and die. And I did fall down. We had just passed through a soft, wet place, and it seemed to me that I was frozen. And I fell down on my dark, cold way, unable to proceed. I was then carried into a slave's cabin, and allowed to warm and rest. It was nearly midnight when I arrived, with my conducter, at my place of exile and suffering. And certainly no heart could be more entirely wretched than I was when I threw my weary, aching body on my cold, hard bed.

The next morning I was called into the presence of Mr. Jones, my new master, and my work was assigned to me. I was to take care of the old gray horse, kept for the use of the family when they wished to ride out, to fetch water from the spring to the house, to go on errands to my master's store, to clean the boots and shoes belonging to the white members of the family, and to the white visitors, to sweep the rooms, and to bring wood from the wharf on my head for the fires at the house and store. From the first dawn of day till ten and eleven, and sometimes twelve at night, I could hardly find one moment's time for rest. And, oh, how the memory of that year of constant toil and weariness is imprinted on my heart, an impression of appalling sorrow. My dreams are still haunted with the agony of that year. I had just been torn from my home ; my yearning heart was deprived of the sweet sympathy of those to whose memory I then clung, and to whom my heart still turns with irrepressible and unutterable longings. I was torn from them and put into a circle of cold, selfish and cruel hearts, and put then to perform labors too great for my young strength. And yet I lived through that year, just as the slave lives on through weary years of suffering, on which no ray of light shines, save that which hope of a better, happier future gives even to the desolate bondman. I lived through it, with all its darkness and sorrow. That year I received my first whipping. I had failed one day to finish my allotted task. It seemed to me that I had done my best ; but somehow, that day, thoughts of home came so fresh and tender into my mind, and, along with these thoughts, a sense of my utter hopeless desolation came in and took such a strong hold of my heart, that I sank down a helpless, heart-broken child. My tasks for that day were neglected. The next morning my master made me strip off my shirt, and then whipped me with a cowhide till the blood ran trickling down upon the floor. My master was very profane, and with dreadful oaths, he assured me that there was only one way for me to avoid a repetition of this terrible discipline, and that was to do my tasks every day, sick or well.

And so this year went by, and my duties were changed, and my lot was made a little easier. The cook, Fanny, died, and I was put into her place. I still had to get wood, and keep the fires in the house, and, after the work of cooking, setting the table, clearing away and washing the dishes, there was always something to be done for my mistress. I got but little time to rest; but I got enough to eat, which I had not done the year before. I was by the comfortable fire a good part of the cold winter weather, instead of being exposed to the cold and wet, without warm clothing, as I had been the year before, and my labor was not so hard the second year as it had been the first.

My mistress complained of me at length, that I was not so obedient as I ought to be, and so I was taken from the house into the store. My business there was to open and sweep out the store in the morning, and get all the things ready for the accommodation of customers who might come in during the day. Then I had to bring out and deliver all heavy articles that might be called for during the day, such as salt, large quantities of which were sold in the store, ship stores, grain, &c. I had also to hold myself ready to run on any errand my master or clerk, David Cogdell, might wish to send me on. While Cogdell remained in the store, I enjoyed a *gleam* of happiness. He was very kind to me, never giving me a cross word or sour look; always ready to show me how to do anything which I did not understand, and to perform little acts of kindness to me. His condescension to me, a poor, despised, homeless and friendless slave, and his tenderness to me, while all others were severe and scornful, sank down a precious bond of grateful emotion into my desolate heart. I seemed to be lifted up by this noble friend at times, from the dark despair which had settled down upon my life, and to be joined once more to a living hope of future improvement in my sad lot. Should these simple words ever meet the eye of David Cogdell, let them assure him of my fervent gratitude and affection for his goodness to me. Let them tell him how infinitely precious to my mourning heart, then and now, his generous treatment and noble kindness to a despised and unhappy boy. And let them say to him, "My early and true friend, Tommy, the poor slave boy, whom you blessed with unfailing kindness, has now grown to be a man, and has run away from the dark misery of bondage. And now, when he calls upon his Father in Heaven to pour out rich blessings on the few friends who have aided him, then David Cogdell is remembered with fond and fervent affection." David was one of the few who always regarded the feelings and happiness of others as earnestly as his own ; who find their own happiness in making the unfortunate happy by sympathy and kindness, and who would suffer any loss rather than do injustice to the poor and defenceless. I often wondered how there could be such a difference in the character of two men, as there was between that of my master and my friend and benefactor, David Cogdell. And I often wished that I might pass into the hands of such a man as he was. But his kindness and generosity to the poor slaves was very offensive to my master, and to other slaveholders ; and so, at length, Mr. Jones turned him off, though he was compelled to acknowledge, at the same time, that he was the most trustworthy and valuable assistant he ever had in his store.

After my master dismissed Mr. C., he tried to get along with me alone in the store. He kept the books and waited upon the most genteel of his customers, leaving me to do the rest of the work. This went on six months, when he declared that he could not bear this confinement any longer ; and so he got a white boy to come and enter as clerk, to stay till he was of age. James Dixon was a poor boy about my own age, and when he came into the store, could hardly read or write. He was accordingly engaged a part of each day with his books and writing. I saw him studying, and asked him to let me see his book. When he felt in a good humor, James was very kind and obliging. The great trouble with him was, that his fits of ill-humor were much more frequent than his times of good feeling. It happened, however, that he was on good terms with himself when I asked him to show me his book, and so he let me take it and look at it, and he answered very kindly many questions which I asked him about books and schools and learning. He told me that he was trying to get learning enough to fit him to do a good business for himself after he should get through with Mr. Jones. He told me that a man who had learning would always find friends, and get along very well in the world without having to work hard, while those who had no learning would have no friends and be compelled to work very hard for a poor living all their days. This was all new to me, and furnished me topics for wondering thought for days afterwards. The result of my meditations was, that an intense burning desire to learn to read and write took possession of my mind, occupying me wholly in waking hours, and stirring up earnest thoughts in my soul even when I slept. The question which then took hold of my whole consciousness was, How can I get a book to begin? James told me that a spelling-book was the first one necessary in getting learning. So I contrived how I might obtain a spelling-book. At length, after much study, I hit upon this plan : I cleaned the boots of a Mr. David Smith, Jr., who carried on the printer's business in Wilmington, and edited the Cape Fear Recorder. He had always appeared to me a very kind man. I thought I would get him to aid me in procuring a spelling-book. So I went one morning, with a beating heart, into his office, and asked him to sell me a spelling-book. He looked at me in silence and with close attention for some time, and asked me what I wanted. I told him I wanted to learn to read. He shook his head, and replied, " No, Thomas, it would not answer for me to sell you a book to learn out of; you will only get yourself into trouble if you attempt it ; and I advise you to get that foolish notion out of your head as quickly as you can."

David's brother, Peter Smith, kept a book and stationery store under the printing-office, and I next applied to him for a book, determined to persevere till I obtained this coveted treasure. He asked me the same question that his brother David had done, and with the same searching, suspicious look. · By my previous repulse I had discovered that I could not get a spelling-book if I told what I wanted to do with it, and so I told a lie, in order to get it. I answered, that I wanted it for a white boy, naming one that lived at my master's, and that he had given me the money to get it with, and had asked me to call at the store and buy it. The book was then handed out to me, the money taken in return, and I left, feeling very rich with my long-desired treasure. I got out of the store, and, looking around to see that no one observed me, I hid my book in my bosom, and hurried on to my work, conscious that a new era in my life was opening upon me through the possession of this book. That counsciousness at once awakened new thoughts, purposes, and new hopes, a new life, in fact, in my experience. My mind was excited. The words spoken by James Dixon of the great advantages of learning, made me intensely anxious to learn. I was a slave ; and I knew that the whole community was in league to keep the poor slave in ignorance and chains. Yet I longed to be free, and to be able to move the minds of other men by my thoughts. It seemed to me now, that, if I could learn to read and write, this learning might—nay, I really thought it would, point out to me the way to freedom, influence, and real, secure happiness. So I hurried on to my master's store, and, watching my opportunity to do it safe from curious eyes, I hid my book with the utmost care, under some liquor barrels in the smoke house. The first opportunity I improved to examine my book. I looked it over with the most intent eagerness, turned over its leaves, and tried to discover what the new and strange characters which I saw in its pages might mean. But I found it a vain endeavor. I could understand a picture, and from it make out a story of immediate interest to my mind. But I could not associate any thought or fact with these croooked letters with which my primer, was filled. So the next day I sought a favorable moment, and asked James to tell me where a scholar must begin in order to learn to read, and how. He laughed at my ignorance, and taking his spelling-book, showed me the alphabet in large and small letters on the same page. I asked him the name of the first letter, pointing it out; he told me A; so of the next, and so on through the alphabet. I managed to remember A and B, and I studied and looked out the same letters in many other parts of the book. And so I fixed in a tenacious memory the names of the first two letters of the alphabet. But I found I could not get on without help, and so I applied to James again to show me the letters and tell me their names. This time he suspected me of trying to learn to read myself, and he plied me with questions till he ascertained that I was, in good earnest, entering upon an effort to get knowledge. At this discovery he manifested a good deal of indignation. He told me, in scorn, that it was not for such as *me* to try to improve, that *I* was a *slave*, and that it was not proper for *me* to learn to read. He threatened to tell my master, and at length, by his hard language, my anger was fully aroused, and I answered taunt with taunt. He called me a poor, miserable nigger; and I called him a poor, ignorant white servant boy. While we were engaged in loud and angry words, of mutual defiance and scorn, my master came into the store. Mr. Jones had never given me a whipping since the time I have already described, during my first year of toil, want and suffering in his service. But he now caught me in the unpardonable offence of giving saucy language to a white boy, and one, too, who was in his employ. Without stopping to make any inquiries, he took down the cowhide, and gave me a severe whipping. He told me never talk back to a white man on pain of flogging. I suppose this law or custom is universal at the south. And I suppose it is thought necessary to enforce this habit of obsequious submission on the part of the colored people to the whites, in order to maintain their supremacy over the poor, outraged slaves.

I will mention, in this connection, as illustrative of this cruel custom, an incident which I saw just before I ran away from my chains.   A little colored boy was carrying along through Wilmington a basket of food. His name was Ben, and he belonged to Mrs. Runkin, a widow lady. A little mischievous white boy, just about Ben's age and size, met him, and purposely overturned the little fellow's basket, and scattered his load in the mud.   Ben, in return for this wanton act, called him some hard name, when the white boy clinched him to throw him down with the scattered fragments upon his basket in the mud.   Ben resisted, and threw down the white boy, proving to be the stronger of the two. Tom Myers, a young lawyer of Wilmington, saw the contest, and immediately rushing out, seized little Ben and dragged him into the store opposite the place of battle. He sent out to a saddler's shop, procured a cowhide, and gave the little fellow a tremendous flogging, for the daring crime of resisting a white boy who had wantonly invaded his rights.   Is it any wonder that the spirit of self-respect of the poor ignorant slave is broken down by such treatment of unsparing and persevering cruelty ?

I was now repulsed by James, so that I could hope for no assistance from him in learning to read. But I could not go on alone. I must get some one to aid me in starting, or give up the effort to learn. This I could not bear to do. I longed to be able to read, and so I cast about me to see what I could do next. I thought of a kind boy at the bake-house, near my own age. I thought he would help me, and so I went to him, showed my book, and asked him to teach me the letters. He told their names, and went over the whole alphabet with me three times. By this assistance I learned a few more of the letters, so that I could remember them afterwards when I sat down alone and tried to call them over. I could now pick out and name five or six of the letters in any part of the book. I felt then that I was getting along, and the consciousness that I was making progress, though slow and painful, was joy and hope to my sorrowing heart, such as I never felt before. I could not with safety go to the bake-house, as there I was exposed to detection by the sudden entrance of customers or idlers. I wanted to get a teacher who would give me a little aid each day, and now I set about securing this object. As kind Providence would have it, I easily succeeded, and on this wise: A little boy, Hiram Bricket, ten years old, or about that age, came along by the store one day, on his way home from school, while my master was gone home to dinner, and James was in the front part of the store. I beckoned to Hiram to come round to the back door; and with him I made a bargain to meet me each day at noon, when I was allowed a little while to get my dinner, and to give me instruction in reading. I was to give him six cents a week. I met him the next day at his father's stable, the place agreed upon for our daily meeting; and, going into one of the stalls, the noble little Hiram gave me a thorough lesson in the alphabet. I learned it nearly all at that time, with what study I could give it by stealth during the day and night. And then again I felt lifted up and happy.

I was permitted to enjoy these advantages, however, but a short time. A black boy, belonging to Hiram's father, one day discovered our meeting and what we were doing. He told his master of it, and Hiram was at once forbidden this employment. I had then got along so that I was reading and spelling in words of two syllables. My noble little teacher was very patient and faithful with me, and my days were passing away in very great happiness under the consciousness that I was learning to read. I felt at night, as I went to my rest, that I was really beginning to be a *man*, preparing myself for a condition in life better and higher, and happier than could belong to the ignorant *slave*. And in this blessed feeling I found, waking and sleeping, a most precious happiness.

After I was deprived of my kind little teacher, I plodded on the best way I could myself, and in this way I got into words of five syllables. I got some little time to study by daylight in the morning, before any of my master's family had risen.   I got a moment's opportunity at noon, and sometimes at night.   During the day I was in the back store a good deal, and whenever I thought I could have five minutes to myself, I would take my book and try to learn a little in reading and spelling.   If I heard James, or master Jones, or any customer coming in, I would drop my book among the barrels, and pretend to be very busy shovelling the salt or doing some other work.   Several times I came very near being detected.   My master suspected something, because I was so still in the back room, and a number of times he came very slily to see what I was about. But at such times I was always so fortunate as to hear his tread or see his shadow on the wall in time to hide away my book.

When I had got along to words of five syllables, I went to see a colored friend, Ned Cowan, whom I knew I could trust.   I told him I was trying to learn to read, and asked him to help me a little.   He said he did not dare to give me any instruction, but he heard me read a few words, and then told me I should learn if I would only persevere as nobly as I had done thus far.   I told him *how* I had got along, and what difficulties I had met with.   He encouraged me, and spoke very kindly of my efforts to improve my condition by getting learning.   He told me I had got along far enough to get another book, in which I could learn to write the letters, as well as to read.   He told me where and how to procure this book.   I followed his directions, and obtained another spelling-book at Worcester's store, in Wilmington.   Jacob showed me a little about writing.   He set me a copy, first of straight marks.   I now got me a box which I could hide under my bed, some ink, pens, and a bit of candle.   So, when I went to bed, I pulled my box out from under my cot, turned it up on end, and began my first attempt at writing.   I worked away till my candle was burned out, and then laid down to sleep.   Jacob next set me a copy which he called pot

hooks ; then, the letters of the alphabet. These letters
were also in my new spelling-book, and according to
Jacob's directions, I set them before me for a copy, and
wrote on these exercises till I could form all the letters
and call them by name. One evening I wrote out my
name in large letters—THOMAS JONES. This I
carried to Jacob, in a great excitement of happiness,
and he warmly commended me for my perseverance and
diligence.

About this time, I was at the store early one morning, and, thinking I was safe from all danger for a few
minutes, had seated myself in the back store, on one of
the barrels, to study in my precious spelling-book.
While I was absorbed in this happy enterprise, my master came in, much earlier than usual, and I did not hear
him. He came directly into the back store. I saw his
shadow on the wall, just in time to throw my book over
in among the barrels, before he could see what it was,
although he saw that I had thrown something quickly
away. His suspicion was aroused. He said that I had
been stealing something out of the store, and fiercely
ordered me to get what I threw away just as he was
coming in at the door. Without a moment's hesitation,
I determined to save my precious book and my future
opportunities to learn out of it. I knew if my book
was discovered that all was lost, and I felt prepared for
any hazard or suffering rather than give up my book
and my hopes of improvement. So I replied at once
to his questions, that I had not thrown any thing away;
that I had not stolen anything from the store ; that I
did not have anything in my hands which I could throw
away when he came in. My master declared in a high
passion, that I was lying, and ordered me to begin and
roll away the barrels. This I did ; but managed to
keep the book slipping along so that he could not see
it, as he stood in the door-way. He charged me again
with stealing and throwing something away, and I
again denied the charge. In a great rage, he got down
his long, heavy cow-hide, and ordered me to strip off

my jacket and shirt, saying, with an oath, "I will make you tell me what it was you had when I came." I stripped myself, and came forward, according to his directions, at the same time denying his charge with great earnestness of tone, and look, and manner. He cut me on my naked back, perhaps thirty times, with great severity, making the blood flow freely. He then stopped, and asked me what I had thrown away as he came in. I answered again that I had thrown nothing away. He swore terribly ; said he was certain I was lying, and declared he would kill me if I did not tell him the truth. He whipped me the second time with greater severity, and at greater length than before. He then repeated his question, and I answered again as before. I was determined to die, if I could possibly bear the pain, rather than give up my dear book. He whipped me the third time, with the same result as before, and then seizing hold of my shoulders, turned me round as though he would inflict on my quivering flesh still another scourging, but he saw the deep gashes he had already made, and the blood already flowing under his cruel infliction ; and his stern purpose failed him. He said, "Why, Tom, I didn't think I had cut you so bad," and saying that, he stopped, and told me to put on my shirt again. I did as he bade me, although my coarse shirt touching my raw back put me to a cruel pain. He then went out, and I got my book and hid it safely away before he came in again. When I went to the house, my wounds had dried, and I was in an agony of pain. My mistress told the servant girl, Rachel, to help me off with my shirt, and to wash my wounds for me, and put on to them some sweet oil. The shirt was dried to my back so that it could not be got off without tearing off some of the skin with it. The pain, upon doing this, was greater even than I had endured from my cruel whipping. After Rachel had got my shirt off, my mistress asked me what I had done for which my master had whipped me so severely. I told her he had accused me of stealing when I had not, and then had whipped me to make me own it.

While Rachel was putting on the sweet oil my master came in, and I could hear mistress scolding him for giving me such an inhuman beating, when I had done nothing. He said in reply, that Tom was an obstinate liar, and that was the reason why he had whipped me.

But I got well of my mangled back, and my book was still left. This was my best, my constant friend. With great eagerness, I snatched every moment I could get, morning, noon and night, for study. I had begun to read ; and, oh, how I loved to study, and to . dwell on the thoughts which I gained from reading. About this time, I read a piece in my book about God. It said that " God, who sees and knows all our thoughts, loves the good and makes them happy ; while he is angry with the.bad, and will punish them for all their sins." This made me feel very unhappy, because I was sure I was not good in the sight of God. I thought about this, and could'nt get it out of my mind a single hour. So I went to James Galley, a colored man, who exhorted the slaves sometimes on Sunday, and told him my trouble, asking, " what shall I do ? " He told me about Jesus, and told me I must pray the Lord to forgive me and help me to be good and happy. So I went home, and went down cellar and prayed, but I found no relief, no comfort for my unhappy mind. I felt so bad that I could not study my book. My master saw that I looked very unhappy, and he asked me what ailed me. I did not dare *now* to tell a lie, for I wanted to be good, that I might be happy. So I told my master just how it was with me ; and then he swore terribly at me, and said he would whip me if I did not give over praying. He said there was no heaven and no hell, and that Christians were all hypocrites, and that there was nothing after this life, and that he would not permit me to go moping round, praying and going to the meetings. I told him I could not help praying, and then he cursed me in a great passion, and declared he would whip me if he knew of my going on any more in that foolish way. The next night I was to a meet ing, which was led by Jack Cammon, a free colored man, and a class leader in the Methodist Church. I was so much overcome by my feelings, that I staid very late. They prayed for me, but I did not yet find any relief; I was still very unhappy. The next morning, my master came in, and asked me if I went the night before to the meeting. I told him the truth. He said, "didn't I tell you I would whip you if you went nigh these meetings, and did n't I tell you to stop this foolish praying?" I told him he did, and if he would, why, he might whip me, but still I could not stop praying, because I wanted to be good, that I might be happy and go to heaven. This reply made my master very angry. With many bitter oaths, he said he had promised me a whipping, and now he should be as good as his word. And so he was. He whipped me, and then forbade, with bitter threatenings, my praying any more, and especially my going again to meeting. This was Friday morning. I continued to pray for comfort and peace. The next Sunday I went to meeting. The minister preached a sermon on being born again, from the words of Jesus to Nicodemus. All this alone deepened my trouble of mind. I returned home very unhappy. Collins, a free man of color, was at the meeting, and told my master that I was there. So, on Monday morning my master whipped me again, and once more forbade my going to meetings and praying. The next Sunday there was a class meeting, led by Binney Pennison, a colored free man. I asked my master, towards night, if I might go out. I told him I did not feel well. I wanted to go to the class meeting. Without asking me where I was going, he said I might go. I went to the class. I staid very late, and I was so overcome by my feelings, that I could not go home that night. So they carried me to Joseph Jones' cabin, a slave of Mr. Jones. Joseph talked and prayed with me nearly all night. In the morning I went home as soon as it was light, and, for fear of master, I asked Nancy, one of the slaves, to go up into mistress's room and get the store key for me, that I might go and open the store. My master told her to go back and tell me to come up. I obeyed with many fears. My master asked me where I had been the night before. I told him the whole truth. He cursed me again, and said he should whip me for my obstinate disobedience ; and he declared he would kill me if I did not promise to obey him. He refused to listen to my mistress, who was a professor, and who tried to intercede for me. And, just as soon as he had finished threatening me with what he would do, he ordered me to take the key and go and open the store. When he came into the store that morning, two of his neighbors, Julius Dumbiven, and McCauslin, came in too. He called me up and asked me again where I staid last night. I told him with his boy, Joseph. He said he knew that was a lie ; and he immediately sent off for Joseph to confirm his suspicions. He ordered me to strip off my clothes, and, as I did so, he took down the cow-hide, heavy and stiff with blood which he had before drawn from my body with that cruel weapon, and which was congealed upon it. Dumbiven professed to be a Christian, and he now came forward, and earnestly interceded for me, but to no purpose, and then he left. McCauslin asked my master, if he did not know that a slave was worth more money after he became pious than he was before. And why then, he said, should you forbid Tom going to meetings and praying ? He replied, that religion was all a damned mockery, and he was not going to have any of his slaves praying and whining round about their souls. McCauslin then left. Joseph came and told the same story about the night before that I had done ; and then he began to beg master not to whip me. He cursed him and drove him off. He then whipped me with great severity, inflicting terrible pain at every blow upon my quivering body, which was still very tender from recent lacerations. My suffering was so great, that it seemed to me I should die. He paused at length, and asked me would I mind him and stop praying. I told him I could not promise him not to pray any more, for I felt that I must and should pray as long as I lived. "Well, then, Tom," he said, "I swear that I will whip you to death." I told him I could not help myself, if he was determined to kill me, but that *I must pray while I lived.* He then began to whip me the second time, but soon stopped, threw down the bloody cowhide, and told me to go wash myself in the river, just back of the store, and then dress myself, and if I was determined to be a fool, why, I must be one. My mistress now interceded earnestly for me with my cruel master. The next Sabbath was love feast, and I felt very anxious to join in that feast. This I could not do without a paper from my master, and so I asked mistress to help me. She advised me to be patient, and said she would help me all she could. Master refused to give any paper, and so I could not join in the love feast the next day.

On the next Friday evening, I went to the prayer meeting. Jack Cammon was there, and opened the meeting with prayer. Then Binney Pennison gave out the sweet hymn, which begins in these words:

> " Come ye sinners, poor and needy,
>   Weak and wounded, sick and sore."

I felt that it all applied most sweetly to my condition, and I said in my heart, *I* will come *now* to Jesus, and *trust* in him. So when those who felt anxious were requested to come forward and kneel within the altar for prayer, *I* came and knelt down. While Jacob Cammon was praying for me, and for those who knelt by my side, my burden of sorrow, which had so long weighed me down, was removed. I felt the glory of God's love warming my heart, and making me very happy. I shouted aloud for joy, and tried to tell all my poor slave brothers and sisters, who were in the house, what a dear Saviour I had found, and how happy I felt in his precious love. Binney Pennison asked me if I could forgive my master. I told him I could, and

2

did, and that I could pray God to forgive him, too, and make him a good man. He asked me if I could tell my master of the change in my feelings. I told him I should tell him in the morning. " And what," he said, " will you do if he whips you still for praying and going to meeting ? " I said I will ask Jesus to help me to bear the pain, and to forgive my master for being so wicked. He then said, " Well, then, Brother Jones, I believe that you are a Christian."

A good many of us went from the meeting to a brother's cabin, where we began to express our joy in happy songs. The palace of General Dudley was only a little way off, and he soon sent over a slave with orders to stop our noise, or he would send the patrolers upon us. We then stopped our singing, and spent the remainder of the night in talking, rejoicing and pray- ing. It was a night of very great happiness to me. The contrast between my feelings then, and for many weeks previous, was very great. Now, all was bright and joyous in my relations towards my precious Saviour. I felt certain that Jesus was my Saviour, and in this blessed assurance a flood of glory and joy filled my happy soul. But this sweet night passed away, and, as the morning came, I felt that I must go home, and bear the *slave's heavy* cross. I went, and told my mis- tress the blessed change in my feelings. She promised me what aid she could give me with my master, and enjoined upon me to be patient and very faithful to his interest, and, in this way, I should at length wear out his opposition to my praying and going to meeting.

I went down to the store in a very happy state of mind. I told James my feelings. He called me a fool, and said master would be sure to whip me. I told him I hoped I should be able to bear it, and to for- give master for his cruelty to me. Master came down, talked with me a while, and told me he should whip me because I had disobeyed him in staying out all night. He had told me he should whip me if ever I did so, and he should make every promise good. So I began to take off my clothes. He called me a crazy fool, and told me to keep my clothes on till he told me take them off.   He whipped me over my jacket ; but I enjoyed so much peace of mind that I scarcely felt the cow-hide. This was the last whipping that Mr. Jones inflicted upon me.

I was then nearly eighteen years old.   I waited and begged for a paper to join the church six months before I could get it.   But all this time I was cheerful, as far as a slave can be, and very earnest to do all I could do for my master and mistress.   I was resolved to convince them that I was happier and better for being a Christian ; and my master at last acknowledged that he could not find any fault with my conduct, and that it was impossible to find a more faithful slave than I was to him. And so, at last, he gave me a paper to Ben English, the leader of the colored members, and I joined the love feast, and was taken into the church on trial for six months.   I was put into Billy Cochrane's class.   At the expiration of six months, I was received into the Church in full fellowship, Quaker Davis' class.   I remained there three years. My master was much kinder after this time than he had ever been before ; and I was allowed some more time to myself than I had been before.   I pursued my studies as far as I could, but I soon found the utter impossibility of carrying on my studies as I wished to do.   I was a slave, and all avenues to real improvement I found guarded with jealous care and cruel tenacity against the despised and desolated bondman.

I still felt a longing desire to improve, to be free, but the conviction was getting hold of my soul that I was only struggling in vain when seeking to elevate myself into a manly and happy position.   And now my mind was fast sinking into despair.   I could read and write, and often enjoyed much happiness in poring over the very few books I could obtain ; and especially, at times, I found great peace in reading my old worn Testament. But I wanted now that hope which had filled my mind with such joy when I first began to learn to read.   I found much happiness in prayer.   But here, also, my mind labored in sadness and darkness much of the time. I read in my Testament that Jesus came from the bright heaven of his glory into this selfish and cruel world to seek and to save the lost. I read and pondered with deep earnestness on the blessed rule of heavenly love which Jesus declared to be the whole of man's duty to his fellow : each to treat his brother as he would be treated. I thought of the command given to the followers of the loving Savior, to teach all nations to obey the blessed precepts of the gospel. I considered that eighteen hundred years had gone by since Jesus plead for man's redemption and salvation, and, going up to heaven, had left His work of mercy to be finished by His children, and then I thought that I and thousands of my brothers and sisters, loving the Lord and pressing on to a blessed and endless home in His presence, were slaves—branded, whipped, chained ; deeply, hopelessly degraded,—thus degraded and outraged, too, in a land of Bibles and Sabbaths and Churches, and by professed followers of the Lord of Love. And often, such thoughts were too much for me. In an agony of despair, I have at times given up prayer and hope together, believing that my master's words were true, that "religion is a cursed mockery, and the Bible a lie." May God forgive me for doubting, at such times, His justice and love. There was but one thing that saved me from going at once and fully into dark infidelity, when such agony assailed my bleeding heart,—the memory of season's of unspeakable joy in prayer, when Love and Faith were strong in my heart. The sweet remembrance of these dear hours would draw me back to Jesus and to peace in his mercy. Oh that all true Christians knew just how the slave feels in view of the religion of this country, by whose sanction men and women are bound, branded, bought and sold !

About this time my master was taken sick. On Sunday he was prostrated by mortal pains ; and, on Friday the same week he died. He left fifteen slaves ; I was purchased by Owen Holmes for $435. I was then in my twenty-third year. I had just passed through the

darkest season of despairing agony that I had yet
known. This came upon me in consequence of the visit,
which I have already described, to my dear old desolate home.   About this time, too, I entered on a new
and distinct period of life, which I will unfold in another chapter.   I will close this period of sorrow and
shame with a few lines of touching interest to my mind.

> Who shall avenge the slave? I stood and cried;
> The earth, the earth, the echoing sea replied.
> I turned me to the ocean, but each wave
> Declined to be the avenger of the slave.
> Who *shall* avenge the slave? my species cried;
> The winds, the flood, the lightnings of the sky.
> I turned to these, from them one echo ran,
> The *right* avenger of the slave is man.
> Man was my fellow; in *his* sight I stood,
> Wept and besought him by the voice of blood.
> Sternly he looked, as proud on earth he trod,
> Then said, the avenger of the slave is GOD.
> I looked in prayer towards Heaven, a while 'twas still,
> And then methought, God's voice replied, I WILL.

CHAPTER SECOND.

I enter now upon a new development of wrongs and
woes which I, as a slave, was called to undergo.   I
must go back some two or three years from the time
when my master died, and I was sold to Owen Holmes.
The bitterness of persecution which master Jones had
kept up against me so long, because I would try to
serve the Lord, had passed away.   I was permitted to
pray and go to our meetings without molestation.   My
master laid aside his terrible severity towards me.   By
his treatment to me afterwards, he *seemed* to feel that
he had done wrong in scourging me as he had done,
because I could not obey his wicked command, to stop
praying and keep away from the meetings.   For, after
the time of my joining the Church, he allowed me to
go to all the meetings, and granted me many other little
favors, which I had never before received from him.
About this time I began to feel very lonely.   I wanted

a friend to whom I could tell my story of sorrows, of unsatisfied longing, of new and fondly cherished plans. I wanted a companion whom I could love with all my warm affections, who should love me in return with a true and fervent heart, of whom I might think when toiling for a selfish, unfeeling master, who shall dwell fondly on my memory when we were separated during the severe labors of the day, and with whom I might enjoy the blessed happiness of social endearments after the work of each day was over.　My heart yearned to have a home, if it was only the wretched home of the unprotected slave, to have a wife to love me and to love. It seems to me that no one can have such fondness of love and such intensity of desire for *home* and home affections, as the poor slave.　Despised and trampled upon by a cruel race of unfeeling men, the bondman must die in the prime of his wretched life, if he finds no refuge in a dear home, where love and sympathy shall meet him from hearts made sacred to him by his own irrepressible affection and tenderness for them. And so I sought to love and win a true heart in return. I did this too, with the full knowledge of the desperate agony that the slave husband and father is exposed to.　Had I not seen this in the anguish of my own parents? Yea, I saw it in every public auction, where men and women and children were brought upon the block, examined, and bought.　I saw it on such occasions, in the hopeless agony depicted on the countenance of husband and wife there separated to meet no more in this cruel world; and in the screams of wild despair and useless entreaty which the mother, then deprived of her darling child, sent forth.　I heard the doom which stares every slave parent in the face each waking and sleeping hour of an unhappy life.　And yet I sought to become a husband and a father, because I felt that I could live no longer unloved and unloving. I was married to Lucilla Smith, the slave to Mrs Moore. *We called* it and *we considered* it a *true marriage*, although we knew well that marriage was not permitted to the slaves as a sacred right of the loving heart.　Lucilla was seventeen years old when we were married.   I loved her with all my heart, and she gave me a return for my affection with which I was contented.   Oh, God of love, thou knowest what happy hours we have passed in each other's society in our poor cabin.   When we knelt in prayer, we never forgot to ask God to save us from the misery of cruel separation, while life and love were our portion.   Oh, how we have talked of this dreadful fate, and wept in mingling sorrow, as we thought of our desolation, if we should be parted and doomed to live on weary years, away from each other's dear presence.   We had three dear little babes.   Our fondness for our precious children increased the current feeling of love for each other, which filled our hearts.   They were bright, precious things, those little babes ; at least so they seemed to us. Lucilla and I were never tired of planning to improve their condition, as far as might be done for slaves.   We prayed with new fervency to our Father in Heaven to protect our precious babes.   Lucilla was very proud of me, because I could read and write, and she often spoke of my teaching our dear little ones, and then she would say, with tears, " Who knows, Thomas, but *they* may yet be *free and happy ?*"   Lucilla was a valuable slave to her mistress.   She was a seamstress, and very expert at her needle.   I had a constant dread that Mrs. Moore, her mistress, would be in want of money, and sell my dear wife.   We constantly dreaded a final separation. Our affection for each other was very strong, and this made us always apprehensive of a cruel parting. These fears were well founded, as our sorrowing hearts too soon learned.   A few years of very pure and constant happiness for slaves, passed away, and we were parted to meet but once again till we meet in eternity.   Mrs. Moore left Wilmington, and moved to Newbern.   She carried with her my beloved Lucilla and my three children, Annie, four years old ; Lizzie, two and a half years; and our sweet little babe, Charlie.   She remained there eighteen months.   And oh, how lonely and dreary and desponding were those months of lonely life to my crushed heart !   My dear wife and my precious children were seventy-four miles distant from me, carried away from me in utter scorn of my beseeching words. I was tempted to put an end to my wretched life. I thought of my dear family by day and by night. A deep despair was in my heart, such as no one is called to bear in such cruel, crushing power as the poor slave, severed forever from the objects of his love by the cupidity of his brother. But that dark time of despair passed away, and I saw once more my wife and children. Mrs. Moore left Newbern for Tuscaloosa, Ala., and passing through Wilmington on her journey, she spent one night in her old home. That night I passed with my wife and children. Lucilla had pined away under the agony of our separation, even more than I had done. That night she wept on my bosom, and we mingled bitter tears together. Our dear children were baptized in the tears of agony that were wrung from our breaking hearts. The just God will remember that night in the last award that we and our oppressors are to receive.

The next morning Mrs. Moore embarked on board the packet. I followed my wife and children to the boat, and parted from them without a word of farewell. Our sobs and tears were our only adieu. Our hearts were too full of anguish for any other expression of our hopeless woe. I have never seen that dear family since, nor have I heard from them since I parted from them there. God only knows the bitterness of my agony, experienced in the separation of my wife and children from me. The memory of that great woe will find a fresh impression on my heart while that heart shall beat. How will the gifted and the great meet the charge against them at the great day, as the judge shall say to them, in stern displeasure, "I was sick, destitute, imprisoned, helpless, and ye ministered not unto me ; for when ye slighted and despised these wretched, pleading slaves, ye did these acts of scorn against me. Depart ye workers of iniquity."

After my purchase by Owen Holmes, I hired my time at $150 per year, paid monthly. I rented a house of Dr. E. J. Desert.   I worked, loading and unloading vessels that came into Wilmington, and could earn from one dollar to a dollar and a quarter a day.   While my wife and family were spared to bless my home by their presence and love, I was comparatively happy.   But I found then that the agony of the terrible thought, " I am a slave, my wife is a slave, my precious children are slaves," grew bitter and insupportable, just as the happiness in the society of my beloved home became more distinct and abounding.   And this one cup of bitterness was ever at my lips.   Hearts of kind sympathy and tender pity, did I not drain that cup of bitter woe to its very dregs, when my family were carried off into returnless exile, and I was left a heart broken, lonely man !   Can you be still inactive while thousands are drinking that potion of despair every year in this land of schools and Bibles ?   After I parted from my family, I continued to toil on, but not as I had done before. My home was darker than the holds of ships in which I worked.   Its light, the bright, joyous light of love and sympathy and mutual endearments, was quenched. Ah me, how dark it left my poor heart.   It was colder than the winter wind and frost ; the warm sunshine was snatched away and my poor heart froze in its bitter cold.   Its gloom was deeper than the prison or cave could make it.   Was not there the *deserted* chairs and beds, once occupied by the objects of a husband's and a father's love ?   Deserted !   How, and Why ?   The answer, is not the unqualified condemnation of the government and religion of this land ?   I could not go into my cold, dark, cheerless house ; the sight of its deserted room was despair to my soul.   So I worked on, taking jobs whenever I could get them, and working often till nearly morning, and never going to my home for rest till I could toil no more.   And so I passed four years, and I began to feel that I could not live in utter loneliness any longer.   My heart was still and always yearning for affection and sympathy and loving communion.   My wife was torn from me.   I had ceased

2*

to hope for another meeting with her in this world of oppression and suffering ; so I sat down and wrote to Lucilla, that I could live alone no longer, and saying to her the sad farewell, which we could not say when we were sundered. I asked Mary R. Moore to come and cheer me in my desolate home. She became my wife, and, thank God, *she* has been rescued from slavery by the blessing of God and my efforts to save her. She is now my wife, and she is with me to day, and till death parts us, secure from the iron hand of slavery. Three of our dear children are with us, too, in the old Commonwealth. I cannot say they are in a *free* land, for, even here, in the city of Boston, where I am told, is kept the old cradle of liberty, *my* precious children are excluded from the public schools, because their skin is black. Still, Boston is better than Wilmington, inasmuch as the rulers of this place permit me to send my children to any school at all. After my second marriage, I hired my wife of her master, and paid for her time, $48 a year, for three years. We had one child while Mary was a slave. That child is still in chains. The fourth year, by the aid of a white friend, I purchased my wife for $350. We had before determined to try to accomplish this enterprise in order that our dear babes might be free. Besides I felt that I could not bear another cruel separation from my wife and children. Yet, the dread of it was strong and unceasing upon my mind. So we made a box, and, through a hole in the top, we put in every piece of money, from five cents up to a dollar, that we could save from our hard earnings. This object nerved us for unceasing toil, for twenty months or about that time. What hopes and fears beset us as those months wore away ! I have been compelled to hide that box in a hole dug for it, when I knew the patrollers were coming to search my cabin. For well did I know, if they found my box, I should be penniless again. How often have I started and turned in sudden and terrible alarm, as I have dropped a piece of money into my box, and heard its loud ring upon the coin below, lest some prowling enemy should hear it, and steal from me my hoarded treasure. And how often have I started up in my sleep as the storm has beat aloud upon my humble home, with the cry of unspeakable agony in my heart,—" Then, O God, they have taken my box, and my wife and babes are still slaves." When my box was broken open, I still lacked a little of the $350 necessary to buy my wife. The kind friend who had promised to aid me in the contemplated purchase, made up the deficiency, and I became the owner of my wife. We had three children at this time, and, O, how my crushed heart was uplifted in its pride and joy, as I took them in my arms and thought that they were not slaves." These three children are with me and with their mother now, where the slave's chains and whips are heard no more. Oh, how sweet is freedom to man! But doubly dear is the consciousness to the father's heart, made bitter in its incurable woe by the degradation of slavery, that his dear child is never to be a slave! Would to God the fathers of this nation were all possessed of a true consciousness of these things ; for then, surely, they would will and secure the immediate ending of human bondage.

After I had purchased my wife, we still worked hard and saved our earnings with great care, in order to get some property in hand for future use. As I saved my earnings, I got a white man whom I thought my friend (his name I choose to keep back for the present,) to lay it out for me. In this way I became the owner of the cabin in which I lived, and two other small houses, all of which were held in the name of this supposed friend. He held them in his own name for me. A slave cannot hold property. I will here remark that I was de ceived by this man ; and when I ran away from my chains, after sending on my family, I was compelled to sacrifice the whole of this property. I left it, because I could not get my own from his hands, and came off entirely destitute. Thank God, I got away, and now I have no tears to shed over the loss of my houses.

During the winter of 1848-9, a kind lady came and

told me that some white men were plotting to enslave my wife and children again. She advised me to get them off to the free States as quickly and secretly as possible. A lawyer of Wilmington told me they were not safe, unless emancipated by a special act of the Legislature. He was a member of the House, and tried to get through the House a bill for their emancipation. But there was so much ill feeling upon this question that he could not do it. The Legislature threw it aside at once. He then advised me to get them off to the free States as my only course to save them. This I determined to do if possible. I kept a good lookout for a vessel. I found one, and made a bargain with the captain to take on board for New York a free colored woman and her three children. A kind friend gave me a certificate of their freedom to the captain, and I brought my wife and children on board at night, paid the captain $25 for their fare, and staid on the wharf in torturing fear till about sunrise, when I saw the vessel under way. It was soon out of sight. When I went home, threw myself on my knees, and poured out my soul to God, to carry that ship and its precious cargo safely and swiftly on to a free haven, and to guard and guide me soon to a free home with my beloved family. And so I kept on, praying, working, hoping, pining, for nearly three weeks, when I received the happy news that my dear ones were safe with a true-hearted friend in Brooklyn. I had notified him beforehand that they were coming; and now the good and glorious news came that they were safe with Robert H. Cousins, where the slaveholders could trouble them no more. I had arranged with Mary when she left, to come on myself as soon as I could get the money for my houses and land. She was to write to me as though she had gone to New York on a visit, intending to come back, and she was to speak of New York as if she did not like it at all. I knew my master would be very angry when he heard she had gone unbeknown to him, and I thought he would demand to see the letters my wife should get friends in New York to write to me for her; and so I made ready to meet and quiet his suspicions, while I was plotting my own escape. For more than three months I tried to get the money, or part of it for my houses ; but was put off and deceived, till I found I must come off without a cent of the property I had tried so hard to accumulate. I was required to call and see my master every day, because he suspected me of design to run away. He was taken suddenly sick, and then I started for my wife and children. Before I give a narrative of my escape, I will give copies of the letters which passed between me and my wife, while I remained in the land of bondage after her escape. These letters with their post marks, are all in my possession and can be examined by any one who may doubt their authenticity, or the fidelity with which they are here given. The kind friend who has written this narrative for me, has corrected some mistakes in the construction and spelling of these letters, and *some* he has left *uncorrected.* He has also omitted some repetitions ; otherwise they are given as exact copies. I wrote my own letters ; my wife wrote by the help of a friend. I give all my letters, and the two from my wife which I was able to keep. The following was written soon after my wife started for New York.

Wilmington, N. C., July 11, 1849.

MY DEAR WIFE—I write these few lines to inform you that I am well, and hope they may find you and the children well, and all the friends. My dear wife, I long to see you and the children one time more in this world. I hope to see you all soon. Don't get out of heart, for I will come as soon as I can. I hope it will not be long, for God will be my helper, and I feel he will help me. My dear wife you must pray for me that God may help me. Tell John he must be a good boy till I see him. I must not forget sister Chavis. She must pray for me, that God may help me come out. Tell her I say that she must be faithful to God ; and I hope dear wife you will be faithful to God. Tell sister Chavis that Henry will be out soon, and he wants her to keep a good heart and he will send money out to her. Tell her he says she must write to him as soon as she can, for he will not stay long behind her. As soon as he gets his money he will come. I hope to see you all very soon. Tell my Brethering to pray for me, that God may help me to get there safe and make my way clear before me. Help me by your prayers, that God may be with me. Tell brother Robert H. Cousins that he must pray for me ; for I long to meet him one time more in this world. Sister Tucker and husband give their love to you and Sister Chavis, and say that you must pray for them. Dear wife, you may look for me soon. But what way I will come, I can't tell you now. You may look for me in three weeks from now. You must try and do the best you can till I come, You know how it is with me, and how I have to come. Tell the Church to pray for me, for I hope to reach that land if I live, and I want the prayers of all God's children. I can't say any more at this time ; but, I remain your dear husband, till death,

THOMAS JONES.

P. S.—Dear wife, I want you to make out that you don't like New York. When you write to me you must say so. Do mind how you write.

The next letter was written before I had received any certain intelligence of my wife's arrival at New York.

Wilmington, N. C., July 17, 1849.

My Dear Wife—I write to tell you I am well, and I hope these few lines will find you and the children well. I long to see you all one time more. Do pray for me, that God may help me to get to you all. Do ask sister to pray the Lord to help me. I will trust in God, for I know that He is my friend, and He will help me. My dear wife, tell my children I say they must be good till I see them once more. Do give my love to Brother R. H. Cousins, and tell him I hope to meet him in two or three weeks from now. Then I can tell him all I want to say to him. Tell Sister Chavis I say, do not come back to this place till I come. Her husband says he wants her to stay, and he will come on soon. My dear wife, I want you to do the best you can till I come. I will come as soon as I can. You and sister Chavis must live together, for you went together, and you must try to stay together. Do give my love to sister Johnson and husband, and all of my friends. Ask them all to pray for me, that God may be with me in all that I do to meet you all one time more. My dear wife you know how I told you, you must mind how you write your letters. You must not forget to write as if you did not like New York, and that you will come home soon. You know what I told you to do, and now you must not forget it when you write. I will send you some money in my next letter. I have not sold my houses yet, and if I can't sell, I will leave them all, and come to you and the children. I will trust in that God who can help the poor. My dear, don't forget what I told you to do when you write. You know how I have to do. Be careful how you write. I hope to be with you soon, by the help of God. But, above all things, ask all to pray for me, that God may open the way for me to come safe. I hope to be with you soon by the help of the Lord. Tell them if I never come, to go on, and may God help them to go forth to glorious war. Tell them to see on the mountain top the standard of God. Tell them to follow their Captain, and be led to certain victory. Tell them I can but sing with my latest breath, happy, if I may to the last speak His name, preach Him to all, and cry, in death, " Behold the Lamb." Go on, my dear wife, and trust in God for all things. I remain your husband,   THOMAS JONES.

Before I wrote the next, I received the happy news that my wife was safe with Brother Cousins.

Wilmington, N. C., July 25, 1849.

MY DEAR WIFE—Do tell my children they must be good children till I come to them ; and you my dear wife, must do the best you can ; for I don't know how

I will come, but I will do the best I can for you. I hope God will help me, for, if He don't, I don't know what I will do. My dear wife, I have not sold my houses yet, but I will do the best I can. If I had money I would leave all I have and come, for I know the Lord will help me. It is for want of money that I can't come. But I hope, my dear wife, the Lord will help me out. Tell Brother Cousins I hope he and all the people of God will pray for me ; and you, my dear wife, must not forget to pray for me. Ask brother Cousins, if he pleases, to put my children to some school. Dear wife, you know the white people will read your letters to me ; do mind how you write. No one but God knows my heart. Do pray for me. I remain your husband till death.   THOMAS JONES.

P. S.—My dear wife, I received your letter the 24th of July, and was truly glad to hear you arrived safe in New York. Please tell Brother Cousins I will write to him in a few days, and I will send you some money. My dear wife do mind how you write. You must not forget I am in a slave place, and I can't buy myself for the money. You know how it is, and you must tell brother Cousins. I have not sold yet, but if I can't sell, I will come some how, by the help of the Lord. John Holmes is still in my way. I want you to write a letter and say in it, that you will be home in two months, so I can let them read it, for they think I will run away and come to you. So do mind how you write for the Lord's sake.   THOMAS JONES.

The next letter was written to Sister Chavis, who went on to New York, but got disheartened and came back to Wilmington.

Wilmington, N. C., Aug. 4, 1849.

My Dear Sister—I hope to see you in a few days, and all my friends. I hope, dear sister, you will not forget to pray for me, for by the help of God, I will see you in a few days. Your husband is coming on soon, but I will be on before him. I would have been on before now, but I could not get my money. I have had a hard time to get money to leave with. I am sorry to hear that you think we can't get a living where you are. My dear sister, a smart man can get a living anywhere in the world if he try. Don't think we can't live out there, for I know God will help us. You know God has promised a living to all His children. Don't forget that God is ever present, for we must trust Him till death. Don't get out of heart, for I know we can live out there, if any one can. You may look for me before your husband. Don't leave New York before I come, for you know what I told you before you left Wilmington. If you come back to this place before I get off, it will make it bad for me. You know what the white people here are. Please don't come yet. I am your brother in the Lord, till death.

THOMAS JONES.

P.S.—I sent the letter you wrote to Mr. John Ranks. I thought you will wait for a letter from your husband and I hope you will be better satisfied in your mind that we can get a living out there. Your husband has wrote to you last week ; I hope you have got the letter. Oh, that you may trust in God every day, for I know God is your friend, and you must pray night and day, that he may help you. I long to see you one time more in this world. We went into the new Church on the 9th day of this month. God was with us on that day, and we had a good time. Though my time with them is short, I hope God will be with them, and may we all meet in the kingdom at last. So pray for me, my dear sister. Aunt Narvey has been dead nearly four weeks. She died happy in the Lord, and is gone home to rest. I hope we may meet in the kingdom at last. Good night, my dear sister. THOMAS JONES.

The next letter is to my wife and Brother Cousins, and explains itself.

Wilmington, August 7, 1849.

MY DEAR WIFE—I long to see you once more in this world, and hope it will not be very long before I am with you. I am trying, my dear wife, to do all I can to get to you. But I hope you will not forget to mind how you write to me. If you should not mind how you write, you will do me great harm. You know I told you to write that you would be home in two months, or three months at the longest. But in two months I told them you would be home. Now, my dear, you must mind, and don't forget, for you know how it is here ; a man can't say that his soul is his own, that is, a colored man. So do mind how you write to me. Tell Sister Chavis I say she must write to me ; and I hope soon I will write my last letter. I will let you know in my next letter how all things are with me. Dear wife, don't get out of heart, for God is my friend. The will of God is my sure defence, nor earth nor hell can pluck me thence, for God hath spoken the word. My dear wife, in reply to your kind letter, received the second day of this month, I have wrote these few lines. I hope you will pray for me, your dear husband,

THOMAS JONES.

P. S.—To Brother Cousins.—My dear Brother, I hope you will not think hard of me for not writing to you, for you know how it is with me out here. God knows that I would write to you at any time, if it was not for some things. You know the white people don't like for us to write to New York. Now, let me ask your prayers, and the prayers of the Church, and God's children, that I may see you all soon. I know that God is my friend, for He doth my burden bear. Though I am but dust and ashes, I bless God, and often feel the power of God. Oh, my brother, pray for me, who loves you all, for I have found of late much comfort in the word of God's love. When I come where you are, in the work of the Lord, and I hope the time will soon come when the Gospel will be preached to the whole world of mankind. Then go on, dear Brother, and do all you can for the Lord. I hope the Lord will help me to get where you are at work soon. Nothing more, but I remain your brother in the Lord,

THOMAS JONES.

The next is from my wife.

Brooklyn, Aug. 10, 1849.

MY DEAR HUSBAND—I got your kind letter of the 23d July, and rejoiced to hear that you was well. I have been very sick myself, and so has Alexander ; but thanks to the Lord, these lines leave me and the children right well. I hope in God they may find you and my son and my mother, and all enquiring friends, enjoying the same blessings. My dear, you requested me and Mrs. Chavis to stay together, but she has taken other people's advice beside mine and Mr. Cousin's, and has gone away. She started for home before we knew a word of it. She left me on the eighth of this month. Do give my love to Betsey Webb and to her husband. Tell her I am sorry she has not come on before now. I am waiting to see her before I start for home. My dear husband, you know you ought to send me some money to pay my board. You know I don't love to leave in this way with my children. It is true that Brother Cousins has not said anything to me about it. You keep writing that you are going to send it in your next letter ; you know I like to act independent, and I wish you to help me do so now, if you please. Do give my compliments to aunt Moore, and tell her the children all send their love to her. They send their love to you and say they want to kiss you mighty bad. The children send their love to brother Edward. I long to see you, husband. No more at present, but remain your loving wife till death. RYNAR JONES.

The next letter is in answer to the letter from my wife, given above.

Wilmington, N. C., Aug. 12, 1849.

MY DEAR WIFE—I received your paper of the 10th to-day. I am glad to hear that you are well, and the children and friends. I have written to Brother Cousins, and told him to tell you that I had not sold out yet. But I hope to sell in a few days, and then I will send you some money. My dear wife, you know that I will do all I can for you and for my children, and that with all my heart. Do try and wait on me a few days, and

I hope you will see me and the money too. I am try‐
ing to do all I can to sell out, but you know how it is
here, and so does Brother Cousins. I will do all I know,
for I think of you, my dear wife, and the children, day
and night. If I can get my money, I will see you soon,
by the help of God and my good friend, and that is a
woman ; she is waiting for me to come every day. My
dear wife, all I want is money and your prayers, and
the prayers of my friends. I know that God will help
me out of my trouble ; I know that God is my friend,
and I will trust to Him. You wrote to me that Mrs.
Chavis left New York. She has not got home yet. I
hope, dear wife, that you have done all your part for
her. Do give my love to Brother Cousins ; ask him to
pray for me, and all God's people to pray for me, a poor
slave at this time. My dear wife, since I wrote last, I
have seen much of the goodness of the Lord. Pray for
me, that I may see more, and that I may trust in Him.
My dear wife, I want you should pray for me day and
night, till you see me. For, by the help of God, I will
see you all soon. I think now it will be but a few days.
Do give my love to my children, and tell them that I
want to kiss them all. Good night, my dear, I must go
to bed, it is one o'clock at night, and I have a pain in
my head at this time. Do tell Brother Cousins that I
say he must look out for me, on John street, in a few
days. Nothing more, but I remain your husband till
death.   THOMAS JONES.

Letter from my wife.

Brooklyn, August 23, 1849.
MY DEAR HUSBAND—It is with the affectionate
feeling of a wife I received your letter of the 19th inst.
It found me and the children well, and we were glad to
hear that you was well. But we feel very sorry you
have not sold out yet ; I was in hopes you would have
sold by the time you promised, before I got home.
Your letter found Mr. Cousins and his wife very sick.
Mr. C. has not been out of the house going on two
weeks. He was taken by this sickness, so common,

which carries so many people off, but, by the help of God and good attendance, he is much on the mend, and his wife also. You ask how much I pay for board. It is three dollars a week for myself and children. In all the letters you have written to me, you don't say a word of mother or Edward. It makes me feel bad not to hear from them. Husband, I have not paid Mr. Cous: ins any board, and am waiting for you to send me some money. I will pray for you hourly, publicly and privately, and beseech the Almighty God, till I see you again. I shall trust in God ; He will do all things for the best. I am yours till death do us part.

RYNAR JONES.

Last letter to my wife from the land of bondage.

Wilmington, N. C., Aug. 30, 1849.

MY DEAR WIFE—I have been quite sick for three weeks, but, thank God, I am better at this time, and hope these few lines will find you and the children all well. I hope, my dear wife, that you have not got out of heart looking for me ; you know how it is here ; I did think I would have got my money here before this time. But I can't get it, and I will leave all and come to you as soon as I can. So don't get out of heart, my dear wife ; I have a hard trial here ; do pray for me, that the Lord may help me to see you all soon. I think of you day and night, and my dear children ; kiss them for me ; I hope to kiss them soon. Edward is sold to Owen Holmes ; but I think Mr. Josh. Wright will get him from H. I have done all I could for Edward. Don't think of coming back here, for I will come to you or die. But I want you should write one more letter to me, and say you will be home in a month. Mr. Dawson will be in New York next week, and you will see him ; mind how you talk before him, for you know how it is, though he is a friend to me. Now, you must mind what I tell you, my dear wife, for if you don't, you will make it hard for me. Now, my dear wife, you must not come back here for your brother and sister ; they talk too much ; but mind what I say to you, for you know I will do all I can for you ; you must not think that you will not get any money, for you shall have it soon. Don't get out of heart, my dear wife ; I hope I shall see you soon. Nothing more, but I remain your husband till death.

THOMAS JONES.

Soon after despatching this letter, I bargained, while my master lay sick, with the steward of the brig Bell, to stow me away in the hold of the ship, and take me on to New York. I paid him eight dollars, which was all the money I then had or could get. I went into the hold, with an allowance of biscuit and water, and the ship started. She was loaded with turpentine, and I found on the second day that I could not live out the passage there. So I told the steward, and he took me out in a state of great weakness, and stowed me away in one of the state-rooms. Here I was discovered by the captain. He charged me with being a runaway slave, and said he should send me back by the first oppo.tunity that offered. That day a severe storm came on, and for several days we were driven by the gale. I turned to and cooked for the crew. The storm was followed by a calm of several days ; and then the wind sprung up again, and the captain made for port at once. I had reason to suspect, from the manner in which I was guarded, after the ship came to anchor off New York, that the captain was plotting to send me back. I resolved to peril life in a last effort to get on shore. So, while the captain was in the city, and the mate was busy in the cabin mending his clothes, I made a raft of such loose boards as I could get, and hastily bound them together, and committing myself to God, I launched forth upon the waves. The shore was about a mile distant ; I had the tide in my favor, and with its help I had paddled one-fourth the distance, when the mate of the Bell discovered my escape, and made after me in the boat. I waved my old hat for help, and a boat, which seemed to be coming round not far from me, came to my rescue. I was taken on board. They asked me if I was a slave, and told me not to fear to tell the truth, for I was with friends, and they would protect me. I told them my circumstances just as they were. They were as good as their word. When the mate came up they ordered him to keep off, and told him they would prosecute him if he touched me. They took me to Brother Cousins, and gave me a little money and some clothes in addition to all their other kindness.

The meeting with my wife and children I cannot describe. It was a moment of joy too deep and holy for any attempt to paint it. Husbands who love as I have loved, and fathers with hearts of fond, devoted affection, may *imagine* the scene and my feelings, as my dear wife lay sobbing in her joy in my arms, and my three dear little babes were clinging to my knees, crying, "Pa has come: Pa has come." It was the happy hour of my life. I then felt repaid for all my troubles and toils to secure the freedom of my family and my own. O God, would that my other dear ones were here, too. God in mercy speed the day when right shall over might prevail, and all the down-trodden sons and daughters of toil and want shall be free and pious and happy.

I have but little more now to say. The Sabbath after my arrival in Brooklyn, I preached in the morning in the Bethel; I then came on to Hartford. A gentleman kindly paid my passage to that place, and sent me an introduction to a true-hearted friend. I staid in Hartford twenty-four hours; but finding I was pursued, and being informed that I should be safer in Massachusetts than in Connecticut, I came on to Springfield, and from thence to Boston, where I arrived, penniless and friendless, the 7th of October. A generous friend took me, though a stranger, in, and fed and cheered me. He loaned me five dollars to get my dear family to Boston. He helped me to get a chance to lecture in May Street Church, where I received a contribution of $2.58; also in the Sion Church, where I obtained $2.33; and in the Bethel Church, where they gave me $3.53. And so I was enabled to get my family to Boston. Entirely destitute, without employment, I now met with a kind friend, who took me with him to Danvers. I lectured and preached in the Free Evangelical Church, and received most generous and opportune aid. They gave me ten dollars, and by their kindness they lifted up a sinking brother. The next Sabbath evening I lectured in the Wesleyan Church in Boston, and received a contribution of $3.33. During the week following, I was assisted by the pastor of this Church, and by several individual members. The next Sabbath I spent with Brother Flanders, of Exeter, N. H. He gave me a brother's warm welcome. I preached for him in the Wesleyan Church, of which he is pastor, in the morning, and lectured in the evening to a full and attentive house. Here I received a generous contribution of nearly ten dollars. To-morrow is Thanksgiving Day. God will know, and He alone can know, the deep and fervent gratitude and joy with which I shall keep it, as I gather my friends, my dear family, around me to celebrate the unspeakable goodness of God to me, and to speak with swelling hearts of the kindness of the dear friends who have poured upon our sadness and fears the sunlight of sympathy, love and generous aid. May the blessing of Heaven rest down now and forever upon them, is the prayer of their grateful brother, and of his dear family, by their kindness saved from pinching want.

But alas! it was not long before I found that I was not yet free. I had not yet slipped from the chain. The Fugitive Slave Law drove me from my kind friends in New England, and I found that my wanderings were not yet ended. I took refuge in the British Provinces, where God had provided a house of refuge for the houseless, homeless slave. Tribulation and distress, with many kind dealings of Providence and wonderful deliverances, have since been my lot. I hope to be able to tell in another narrative, of my adventures after the close of this story, of the kindness of friends and the goodness of God.

THOMAS H. JONES.

www.ingramcontent.com/pod-product-compliance
Lightning Source LLC
Chambersburg PA
CBHW022202020726
47496CB00008B/2837